The big rain

Françoise [pseud.]

[Seignobosc, Françoise]

Charles Scribner's Sons - New York

It rains and it rains
and it rains.
Jeanne-Marie cannot go
to school.
It is too far from the farm.
To pass the time
she sings a little French song.

Il pleut, il mouille.

C'est la fête à la grenouille.

It rains and it pours.
It's a fine day for frogs.

The little river rises higher
and higher and higher.
And then—it flows over the land.
Little by little, quietly, softly,
the water comes to the farm.
Then, still more quietly,
it comes creeping into the kitchen.
"Up to the second floor,"
Jeanne-Marie's mother cries.
"Help Grandmother first of all.
She can't hurry."

"And then save the animals—
the horse and
the cow,
the pig and
the goat,
the sheep and
the rabbits.
The chickens can save
themselves.
They will fly up
into the trees."

"Get all the animals
to the little hill!"
Jeanne-Marie's father calls.
"They will be safe
on the hill—even if
they are a little cold.
But in the barns
they will be drowned.
Quick!
Now save yourselves!"

And everyone runs back to the house.
The family is together
on the second floor.
What can they do?
No fire in the stove—the wood is
under water.
No more milk—the cow is
on the hill.
No bread—the baker cannot bring it.
Not even water to drink—
no one can get to the well.
It rains and rains.
In the lonely farmhouse
they wait and wait for help.
It rains and it rains and it rains.

Jeanne-Marie does not like it.
Patapon the pet sheep
does not like it.
She looks out of the window.
Nothing but water —>
all around the farm.
Only Madelon
the white duck is happy.
She didn't go to the little hill
like those silly rabbits,
that scared goat,
and that big stupid pig!
Madelon swims here, there,
everywhere. . . . She likes it!

But time goes by and no one comes
to the farm to help.
Madelon does not see her dear little
mistress (Miss) Jeanne-Marie.
Something must be wrong!
She swims here, there, everywhere,
calling, calling . . .
"Quack! Quack! Quack!"
But now, look! A boat is coming.
Madelon swims and swims.
There are two men in the boat.
One has a basket with good things to eat.
"Quack, quack, quack!" calls Madelon.
"This duck looks as smart as a dog,"
says one of the men in the boat.
"Let's follow her!"

So the boat follows Madelon
until it is near the farm.
Jeanne-Marie is on the roof
making distress signals
with a lantern.
Suddenly she hears a triumphant
"Quack, quack, quack!"
Help has come!
She is no longer afraid.

Jeanne-Marie and her family
are happy.
The men have come to take them
to the village.
There they will have
good hot soup.
Patapon goes in the boat, too.
Madelon follows,
but she doesn't quack any more.
She has quacked so much
that her throat hurts.

Soon the rain stops.
The water goes down, down, down.
The animals come down
from the hill.
And the bright Sun shines again.

and the
bright Sun
shines
again.

But there is so much mud
in the houses!
Furniture and clothes are
soaking wet.
In the village school the teacher
says to the children,
"My little friends,
now the flood is over,
there are people who are
in trouble—
old people, sick people
who can't clean the mud
from their houses.
I am counting on you
to help them.
Forward march!"

En avant
marche !...

The children, armed with
shovels and brooms,
try their best
to clean up the houses.
They carry out
the tables and chairs
so that they may dry
in the sun.
They scrub and they scrub
and they scrub.

Jeanne-Marie is very busy
with her broom.
She sweeps with all her might.
Jean-Pierre helps her.
Madelon is resting.

The goat

Cabrette

has caught a little cold.
She coughs.
Her nose runs.
Poor thing!

But the bad days are gone.
Long live the bright Sun!
Vive le gai Soleil!